Worrisome Wilf's
Beastly Bedtime

Written by Séan Baldwin

Illustrated by Martin Gordon

Worrisome Wilf went up to bed
with all sorts of horrible thoughts in his head.
He climbed the stairs slowly,
they creaked with each tread
and he entered his bedroom
struck silent with dread.

He ran to the window, closed his curtains
And peered under his bed to see for certain
if anything awful was waiting that night
Ready to scoff him when he turned out the light.

He checked the wardrobe - above and inside -
He knew these were places where monsters can hide.
Nothing was there, the coast remained clear,
But he still went to bed shivering with fear.

Wilf worked up the courage to turn out the light
And quickly jumped under his bed sheets in fright.
But then he sat up and suddenly cried,
'I'm sure I heard something quite awful outside!'

Like a three-headed Ninja covered in snails,

Scraping a blackboard with long, twisted nails.

Or a skateboarding werewolf trying hard to be champ,

Practising tricks through the night on a ramp.

Maybe, just maybe, it's a rare type of snake,
One that eats shovels, wheelbarrows and rakes,
And when it's done munching these tools for its tea
It'll slide up the drainpipe and start to eat ME!

What if it's aliens landing their ship?
Having got lost on their way to the tip.
They'll be out there all night making noise until dawn,
Dumping their rubbish all over our lawn.

Or perhaps a mad scientist who's kidnapped the Queen
And made a wrong turn in his drilling machine.
He's tunnelled up here and upset all the moles
By leaving my garden all covered in holes!

A banjo-playing cactus
with a hatful of bees?

Perhaps it's a big storm
Called Hurricane Janet!
Her power could rip
Our whole house from the planet!

Shaking and quaking,
Eyes open wide,

He crept to the window
And then looked outside...

But the garden was empty!
All normal and calm.
There was nothing out there
That could bring him to harm.
No nightmarish freaks or thingummies weird;
No sign of the silly old creatures he'd feared.

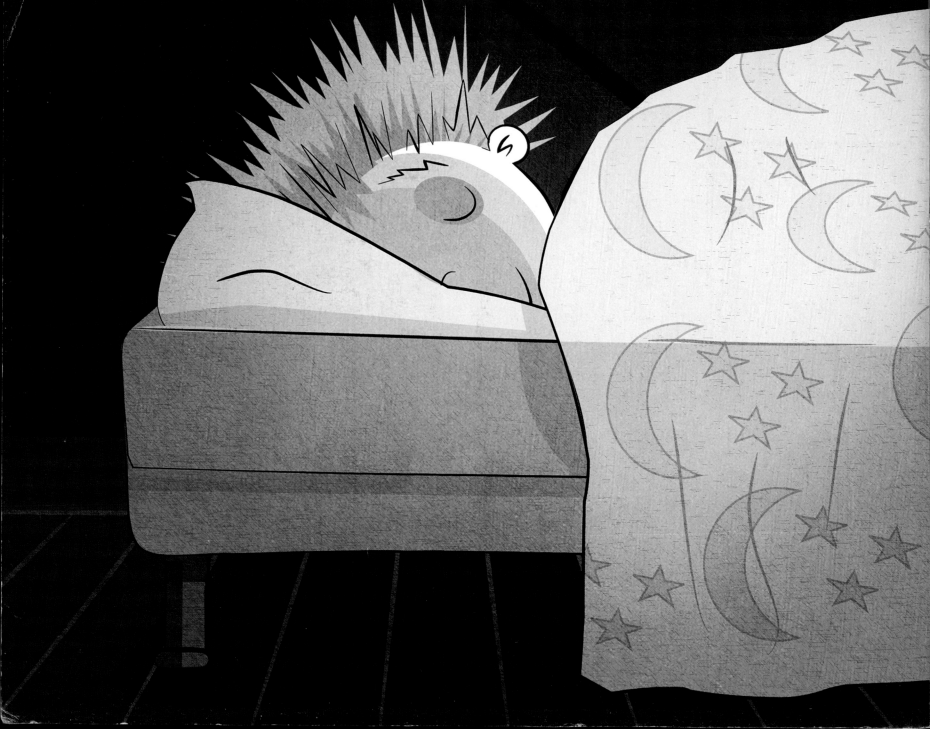

So Worrisome Wilf went back to bed
Without any horrible thoughts in his head.
Sleeping perfectly well, having left them behind,
He smiled at the things he'd made up in his mind.

Thank you to all our supporters and backers who
helped make this book a successful Kickstarter project!

In particular, we'd like to thank the following for their generous contributions:

Anne and George Butterfield
Gary Carter
Maude and Finn Casey
Henry Cobbold
Sue Cruickshank
John and Chris Edwards
Stuart Edwards
Barry Gordon
Lorna Gordon
Stefan Jedrzejewski
Susan Lomax
Nigel Parkinson
Gary Payne
Timothy Robins
Alex Tarling
Emily Truman
Janice Alana Wilson
www.cubeecraft.com

We couldn't have done it without you!

Séan & Martin